The Day Te
Made New Friends

Ann Jungman · Pictures by Toni Goffe

BARRON'S
New York · Toronto

Yesterday my mom took me to a new play group.
I wasn't sure I wanted to go.
"Don't worry," said Mom. "You've got Teddy to
keep you company."

I told Teddy I was worried.
"Why?" asked Teddy.
"I don't know anybody," I told him.

"That's no problem," said Teddy. "Making friends is easy. Just wait and see."

Teddy walked up to another bear.
"I'm new here," said Teddy. "Would you
like to show me around?"

The other bear didn't seem to notice.
"Never mind," said Teddy. "Never mind,
I'll try someone else."

Teddy went up to a doll on a swing.
"Can I give you a push?" he called.
"Yes please," said the doll.

So Teddy pushed the swing
as hard as he could. The doll
went high, high up into the air.
"Do it again," she called to Teddy.

Then Teddy took out a banana.
"Would you like half my banana?" Teddy asked the doll.
I was surprised because he really loves bananas.

"Yes, please," said the doll, and
Teddy gave her the biggest piece.
That doll seemed to like Teddy.

After that the doll was so messy she had to go
and wash. "Oh well," said Teddy, "never mind.
I'll play on my own. There's lots to do here.

What shall I do first? Play in the sand or
make something out of clay? I know,
I'll build a tower."

A panda came to watch Teddy build his tower.
"This is the biggest tower in the world," said Teddy.
"I'll make a bigger one," said the panda.

When the towers were finished Teddy said,
"Let's knock them down."
They both enjoyed that.

Now everyone wanted to make towers. There was
a brown rabbit, and a koala bear, and a clown with
a red hat. They all wanted to play with Teddy.
He really had made a lot of new friends.

Then Teddy waved to me.
"Why don't you come and join in?" he said.
"This game is fun."

So I went and joined in.
Then lots of other children came to play
with Teddy and me.

I decided I liked this play group.

When it was time to go home
I didn't want to leave.